Balamory

BBC

The Monster Party

RED FOX

Oh, hi there! How are you? Today is a play day in Balamory and tonight we're having a Monster Party at the Nursery!

"WOOOO! Someone's left a torch. This will be great for the party! But now . . . we're going to do some face painting!"

Spencer is helping to organize the party, but when he arrives at the café, he gets a terrible fright!

"AARGH! Monsters!"

"Are you looking forward to tonight, Spencer?" laughs Miss Hoolie.
"I sure am! Look, I've even got the apples for the apple-on-a-string game."

"Oh great! Shall we have a practice now? How do we do it?"
"It's easy – you have to get hold of the apple – with your mouth!"

"That's brilliant, Spencer, but it's certainly not easy!" laughs Miss Hoolie. "And all we need now are some lights for the nursery garden."

"Oh no!" says Spencer. "I knew I'd forgotten something! Where *will* I get lights from?"

"Why not try Archie?" Miss Hoolie suggests.
"Good idea! I'll go and see him right now."

"Which colour house is Spencer going to?"

That's right . . . The pink house!
"Oh, hello Spencer, how are you?"
"Not great, Archie, I'm helping Miss
Hoolie with the Monster Party tonight
and I need some lights."

Archie has lots of ideas.

"How about fairy lights?"

"Pretty, but not special enough."

"Torchlight?"

"Too bright."

"Candlelight?"

"Yes, perfect! But we'll need something to put the candles in. And I have to go and sort out my costume!"

"Don't worry, Spencer, leave it to me!"

"Aargh! Spooky! *Now* I'm ready for the party!"

Spencer arrives at the Nursery. "Do you see that? It's a m-m-monster, a glowing monster!"

"I must get help. Quickly. Before the children arrive! PC Plum, help . . . help!" wails Spencer as he dashes off to find Plum.

"Plum! It's OK – it's me, Spencer! I need your help, it's an emergency!"

Spencer shudders.

"Look! Monsters! They're taking over the whole garden!"

"Oh, Spencer, those aren't real monsters," chuckles Plum.
"They're pumpkin lanterns!"

"Wow! Now that *is* clever! A pumpkin with a candle inside!"

Just then, Archie opens the Nursery door. "Gosh, Spencer, you look really spooky!"

"So do your lanterns, Archie. You had me worried there for a minute!"

"Come on, everyone, time to party!" calls Miss Hoolie.

It is the best Monster Party ever!

"So, what was the story in Balamory?

Spencer was helping me with the Monster Party at the Nursery but he had forgotten the lights, so he went to see if Archie could help.

Archie offered to make some lights, and Spencer left to sort out his costume.

Archie made some brilliant pumpkin lanterns, but Spencer thought they were monsters!

So Spencer dashed off to fetch PC Plum. Poor PC Plum thought Spencer was a ghost and got the fright of his life!

Spencer realized his mistake – and after all the frights everyone had a brilliant Monster Party!"

"So that was the story in Balamory!
See you soon, bye!"

THE MONSTER PARTY A RED FOX BOOK 0 09 947579 0
First published in Great Britain by Red Fox, an imprint of
Random House Children's Books by arrangement with the BBC
Red Fox edition published 2004
1 3 5 7 9 10 8 6 4 2

Text and illustrations © Red Fox 2004

BBC © BBC 1996

Balamory © BBC 2002